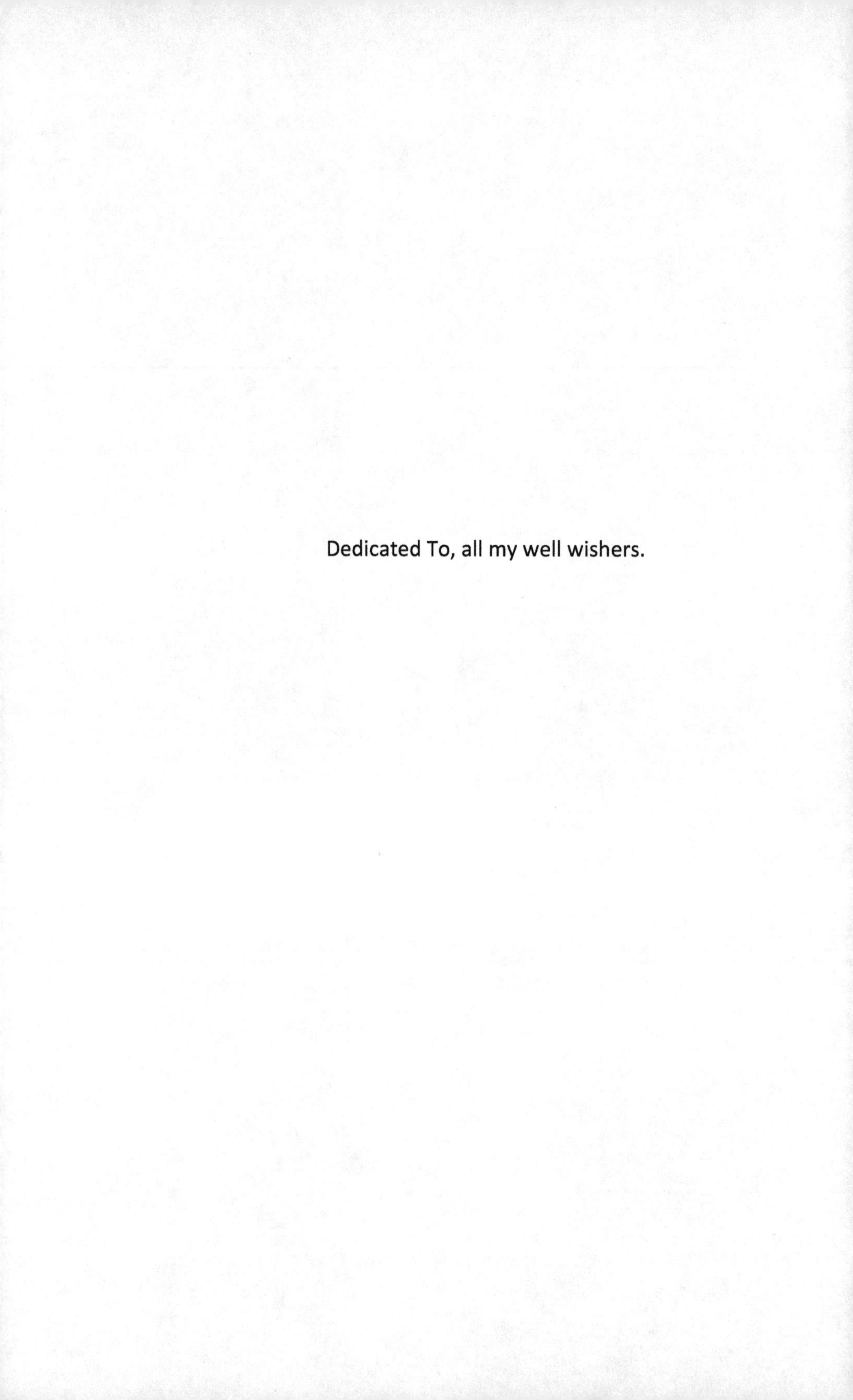

Dedicated To, all my well wishers.

1.

Neelanshu, is sitting in his room, adorned with posters of footballers and rock bands on the walls, led lightings on the ceiling and, beautiful speakers that he got on his 16th birthday ……..preparing for his last exam of the ICSE board examinations.

He toils the pages of the geography book ….. And just stares at the cover for some time …..

6 am in the morning and his mother is already awake

"Uth jaa, revision kar le Nishu….."

"Han bas paanch minute maa…. Mene sab padha hai …"

"Vo to result hi batayega!"

Neelanshu, jumps off from his bed and goes to the study table … and grabs the geography book, goes back to the bed, pulls the quilt and starts studying …

"Go! Have a bath Nishu …"

 His Mother comes in gliding like a bird; holding his crisp uniform … she is always worried about the hectic mornings she has to manage …

He comes out from the washroom flipping his hair ….. dresses up … stands in front of the age old mirror that has been with him since childhood … and the mirror never forgets to remind him of that , as it is already studded with boomer stickers, trump card players, wrestling stars, super cars, bikes…. Cartoons, crayon marks and what not!

"Come … breakfast is ready ….." Says his Father from the dining room ….

He goes, sits down, both have parantha with aachar …. While they also watch news on TV.

"Chalo, bag lelo aaur pencils sharpen kr lena, scale mat bhul jana …. Aaur jao mandir mai bhi eek bar hath jod lo…."

"Haan Papa sab ho gya hai …. Sab ready hai …"

His mother comes with the magical dahi batasha, he eats it ……. Walks, towards the doors of his house…

"All the best Nishu, acche se karna …"

He just smiles and nods …

Now, both father and son sit on their grunty scooter and, make their way to his school on the fiery roads of Patna.

2.

 The piercing sound of bell is heard and, students rush outside the exam hall with the geography paper in their hands, some discuss the answers, while some forget the paper, Neelanshu, and his friends gather at the cordrangle, infront of their school library and, write things on each other's white shirts with colorful sketches and leave the school with a memoir.

"Now what are you planning to take in 11 and 12…?" asks Akriti his batchmate

"Haha kuch socha nahi aabhi … but –"

Interrupts him… says, she is going to take admission in DPS …. With commerce

He smiles, and, wishes all the best and, a good bye to her….

He finally sits at a corner of his school for the last time, in that uniform … and feels the pulse of that place, which would be imbibed in him forever.

He sighs and stands at the school gate, sees his friends waving goodbyes … his father arrives in the scooter asks, how he did the exam … it went well, he says …. and they sit on the scooter…. sound of the scooter fades away.

They reach home … he rushes inside, and throw his bag and tie on the bed …. Unfold his sleeves … and texts his friend, to meet up in the evening for a party.

Sameer and Neelanshu replenish the jar of school memories and laugh out upon all the crisis they went through these years, this point may seem vague to a person who has already passed out of school, but to someone who is changing tracks between schools, tuitions, extracurricular, understands well what crisis here actually means!

They enjoy a meal at "Momo Hub", and talk about music, football, gaming …..

Later, he reaches home ….

His mother asks for dinner, but he says he is full and stuffed …. Further, he goes to his room.

He switches off the lights ,opens the window , just lets the warm breeze enter inside ,lie down on his bed ,stares at the ceiling and goes into the maze of thoughts….. Deep inside somewhere worried about his career ….

Snoring sound is heard.

3.

It is somehow relevant and predictable too, as how a day in a middle class family starts with, there is chaos everywhere; the smell of hot iron fills the room, with jingles of Morning Prayer bells from the mandir, accompanied by whistles of the cooker from the kitchen, the roaring tap sound of that overflowing bucket in the bathroom. Just perfect enough, to make anyone want a cup of morning chai and immerse in the ambience.

Neelanshu leaves the newspaper and sees advertisements of coaching institutes for IIT, Medical -single digit ranks, complemented with professional faces.

 Looks impressive though!

His mother hands him a cup of tea, meanwhile his father leaves for work.

"Nishu, check someone is at the door ….."

"Haan maa wait …." He goes to see whether there's some visitor and opens the door …..

"Namaste sir…! aaiye na andar!"

A man in his 40's, with thick rimmed glasses, and betel stained teeth, a khadi kurta on, makes his way towards their living room.

"Maa, Gopal sir aaye hai …."

His mother arrives … and greets Gopal sir

Gopal sir is a neighbor, and runs tution classes for ICSE and CBSE students …. He knows his job well, be it, teaching, marketing or giving "premium" life lessons to his students.

Well! He is the one, who has tutored Neelanshu, since the child was in his fourth standard, from Math to Science to Hindi, English and other school projects …. Gopal sir was the one to look for.

"Aur kya percent aaega board mai?" Asks Gopal sir, while sipping glucon d

Neelanshu sits like a bride, avoiding eye contact and says 80-90 in a low voice....

"Chalo accha hai …. Paper mai result nikalyenge tution ka to…. thumara bhi photo dalwa denge" and then He laughs with a creking sound ….

"Aur madam ji ,aab 11 aur 12 mai kya dilwa rahe ho? Science hi lega … IIT ya Medical?"

His mother says – "sir aap hi batayie …."

"Dekheye in dono hi field mai bhaut paisa aur izzat hai, aap isko medical karwaiea "Doctor" banaeye!"

"KOTA" bhej deegea .

Gopal sir leaves, and wishes all the best to him… till then, sudden chirping of birds resonates in the sky, following light drops of rain.

4.

"Hazrat Nizamddin" railway station is buzzing with heat of summer, it carries a strange sense of fear within it, and as you enter you are welcomed by the yellow board with the name of station engraved on it …. You see people with tarred bags, cheap memory card sellers, rags, all faces stare at you …. This station hosts thieves, touts, criminals and travelers. It has really got the back of an iron.

Neelanshu, with his father arrives at the station; it appears too noisy, fast and notorious ….

Within every two minutes, an announcement is being made, Doronto express is late by….. And the list goes on and on…

But it's his luck that finally "Kota Jan Shatabdi" is on time …. He enters into the train, B4 B6 are the births they are provided with.

The train carries people, basically of "Rajasthani" and "Marwadi" origin, tanned skinny men in kurtas and women with colorful saris taking care of their kids. The other majority of passengers, consist mostly of students some already studying in coaching institute, as either their jackets or the bags that they carry, boast loud enough the names of the coaching institutes that cannot skip your eyes….the rest are like Neelanshu , waiting to carry that bag or the plain jacket.

"Haan ye hai…. umm b5 b6 aaja beta idhar saara saman aa gaya?"

"Haan Papa…." He keeps the luggage, bigger ones below the seat and the small important bags on the birth itself.

He sits for a while, looks outside …. And, rushes out to purchase a bottle of water …comes inside, sips water and diligently waits for the train to start.

The coolness inside the train is somewhat comforting in contrast to the heat outside, even the noise is now muffled, and windows are the only escape to the outside world …. He stares outside from that blue tinted window of the train and swift movement of the train makes the outside world appear sprinting … he smiles ear to ear, and rests his head on the panes.

Two hours later, refreshed and now filled with energy and excitement, he wakes up … talks on the phone to his Mother.

The train, is about to cross Bharatpur … the Sun, is about to set, and now, the tourists with their guides leave for Bharatpur Sanctuary.

The guy sitting on b9 breaks the silence….

"Hi! My name is Shusheel" utters, somewhat a healthy guy, in his 30's ….

"Hi bhaiya… I am Neelanshu!"

His dad also joins the conversation … says, "aaur beta kesa hai Kota….. isko admission dilane jaa rahe…. aap wahi rehte hai?"

"Haan uncle, mai Kota mai rehta hun, mera ghar Boondi mai bhi hai …."

"Kota…aaaa accha hai, poore India se crowd aata hai idhar …."

"Aaur aap kya karte ho … "

"Mai to bank ki tayaari kar raha hu…" and he smiles.

While crossing Chambal, Kota's thermal power plant towers appear, raw, jeweled with red lights blinking synchronously like sprinting shimmering waves.

"Thermal aagaya matlab, Kota bhi aane wala hai uncle….." says Shushil and they look outside the window.

Thermal towers… stand strong, between blackness of the river Chambal and stillness of the night sky.

5.

Same yellow board is seen, but now, with the name of a totally different and diverse station, "Kota Junction", beautifully written on it with Hindi, English and Urdu calligraphy.

Success and failure itself starts from this place.

The train swiftly stops; people are already queued with their luggage near the exit …… coolies gush inside, contrary to the passengers making way through elbow rowing.

They get off the train, keep the luggage on the platform, breathe calmly and with hands on his waist, Neelanshu gazes slowly and let the feeling of reaching Kota set in.

He is awestruck with huge banners of coaching, pg, hostel mess, food delivery all around the station till then, they are surrounded by autowallahs saying "bhaiya new admission hai?" …… "ya le lia admission?" …. Some say, come to "Rajeev Gandhi Nagar" some, take the name of "Kunhari" while some, say come to "New Rajeev Gandhi Nagar"….

They somehow step out of the station, and stretch their backs after climbing the long staircase……. lines of auto and autowallas rule the station.

 "Saab kaha jana hai …"

"Koi hotel hai ….?"

"Haan aao baitho…kahan admission lena hai engineering ya medical mai?"

 They sit in the auto …. "Medical" says his father.

"11th …12th hai ya 13th hai bacche ka?"

"11th hai iss bar…"

"Hahaha, 2 sal ka plan hai matlab…"

Yeh dekhiye! "Seven Wonders" …. "Kishore Sagar", the autowallh guides them through ……as they are on the way… the huge Indian flag waves off in a welcoming way.

Still! These enormous marvels look tiny, in front of the hoardings that dominate the city.

6.

Next day, they wake up at about 6 am; the room has the sound of ranting fan with air thick and humid.

His father opens the ventilator of the room…. Both take bath, get ready, as today it is going to be a hectic scheduled day, they have to take admission ,then look out for hostels and pg … but first they decide to have breakfast nearby anywhere.

As they step out of the hotel, flocks of students with bags, umbrellas, ID cards …all geared up marching towards their respective coaching centers; the streets are busy with autos, cycles and a horizon of youth. Somehow intriguing at the first sight, this place definitely dances on its own note.

Numerous stalls, line the streets, little carts of food are almost everywhere with "poha" and "kachori" on demand. Students are chatting, and having tea and kachoris on recycled round plates of books question papers with physics, math, chemistry or biology sections, now stained with oil and flakes of, leftovers of kachori and samosa.

They also enjoy the famous khachori of Kota, just observe the place, speak nothing to each other on the way, and then, from the hotel they are ready to explore the city.

7.

10 am, and the temperature is already, 34 degrees Celsius …….

From "Nayapura" where they were staying, they take auto to "Rajeev Gandhi Nagar", where there is the main building of "Ellen Career Institute".

On the way, they see " army area", "g.m.c Kota", "Rajeev Gandhi's statue", sitting, building Nation , on the laptop….. "Cine mall", Kota's "City Mall", loads of "coaching buildings".

This area has two buildings of IIT coaching, and two of Medical, all of different organizations.

"Although summer hits the place hard, but still you can see clouds of umbrellas everywhere."

People are covered from head to toe, to prevent heat wave and tanning.

The building appears to be busy, with students everywhere and parents wrapped up in documents necessary for admission process, the infrastructure, of the place is marvelous, Neelanshu and his Father stand at the queue to fill the admission form ….

After he gets admitted and gets done with all the formalities they drink a glass of sugarcane juice just outside the coaching building and quench their thirst.

At the time of admission, you will see touts, middlemen in streets who will ask you for hostels, pg rooms …. With pamphlets in their hands, and sweet tongues fitted to their jaws ready.

It is baffling to see the streets covered with yellow, white, blue pamphlets all over … these remain in the streets forever, some fly with the occasional spontaneous dusty winds ,while others ,settle down after some time…..

"Hello sir ….mera naam Ramesh Meena hai … aap kaho to hostel dikha dun … ac room hai, Kota ka best, full safe…"

 The guy keeps on hovering, and many like him circle them.

They go with Ramesh ….

He takes them to a hostel in new "Rajeev Gandhi Nagar" …. "Gupta's inn" as the board says

The hostel from outside is painted white, they enter and immediately out of the blue a guy appears and tells them to do entry in a register, shows them rooms, all identical ,with quotes written on the walls, periodic table poster hanging on almost all rooms, and formulas written on the scratched study tables.

"Kitne ke hai ye room ….?"

"Sir 12000 per month …. Electricity bill excluded"

"Balcony wala lenge to … vo 15 ka pad jayega… aaeye mess dekh legeye"

They are escorted to mess … where "Gupta ji", the owner of the hostel is sitting, he wears a striped shirt, with a pen peeping from his pocket … and says, "Lift bhi hai hostel mai yahi le legeye … paani lao sir ke lie" and insists them to eat the mess food …

"Wese bhi… lunch time ho gaya hai…. aap bhi kha leegeye … free hai koi baat nahi "

Then, Neelanshu and his father eat ….. raita gobhi roti and salad.

"Chaleye, aab room ka final kr legea…"

His father says …. "Nahi saab, room ye wale pasand nahi aya bacche ko … shukria"

And as the move out of that hostel …. Gupa ji comes and says "200 rupiya ho gya khane ka …"

Neelanshu's dad pays him with a smile and they leave as there is already enough heat outside, they avoid escalating it up more with arguments.

The autowallah also demands for extra money ….

Now, they realize that they were trapped and get away with the autowallah too.

Neelanshu suggests that now they both should search for hostel in "Rajeev Gandhi Nagar" itself…that would be better as it was also within the radius of his coaching class.

They reach, "Old Rajeev Gandhi Nagar"

This city has hostels, pg, mess like blocks connected, one hostel ends, another starts, another ends, another starts, well in that empty plot, foundation is being laid to build another one ….

They have till now visited more than 20 hostels, and found a loop or the other in each of them ….their legs feel fragile, throats dried, minds fogged …. They buy a bottle of water and sit at a bench roadside to calm down a little.

It is almost 5 pm; they reach near the park of "Old Rajeev Gandhi Nagar" …. And enter into a random hostel, "Mohini Residency" … they are welcomed by a man

"Namaste room dekhna hai …."

"Han… dekhaiye"

"Prajapati room dikhao sir ko, ground wala … sir 2 hi room khali hai ground floor pe "

"Han dekh lete hai…"

"Prajapati", the janitor, shows them the room … it's is not big than the size of an Omni van … but the hostel looks clean hygienic and well organized ….

They sit at the office and fill the form for hostel accommodation …. Pay advance security fees of Rs. 13000. The owner shakes hands with Neelanshu's Father and offers him his visiting card, in which it is written in bold letters…

"Mohini Residency,Old Rajeev Gandhi Nagar, near Ellan Institute Kota."

"Lalit Singh" (owner)

"To Singh saab, aab Nishu ka khayal aap hi ne rakhna hai…." Says his Father to the owner, and they head towards, their hotel room in Nayapura.

Those tiny rooms like cages, with plain walls, vacuum silence in them- either you start living in them or you find a way to escape.

As they enter the hotel room, a message pops out in Neelanshu's mobile phone…

It says,

From-ELLENMEDICAL

Dear Neelanshu (roll num 77899021), batch no mnv59, your classes will commence from 4 April 6 am to 2 pm, Ellen block 1, floor 5, room num 6.

Please, report for orientation session on 3rd April, and collect the ID card, uniform, study material from the Ellen block itself.

All the best!

He empties his bag, stuffed with, pamphlets and visiting cards into the dustbin….. Goes to the washroom talks to his mother and goes to bed

8.

Today ,it is going to be an eventful day first, they have to shift all the luggage into the new hostel room then, they have to attend the orientation ,collect uniform ,ID card and study material from Ellen building … then in the evening he has to see off his father in Kota-Patna from Kota junction … he thinks all of this, in a chronological order , as he takes the shower…

"Chalo ,saaman lelo saara mai neeche reception mai check out karta hun …."

Neelanshu, takes the bags with him descends the stairway; both Father and Son stand waiting for the auto, with "Mohini Residency's" visiting card in hand…. They show it to the auto driver … and make a trail towards…the destination

As he gets off the auto, Prajapati, comes and greets them ….

He picks the luggage, and opens the room …

"Sir safai bhi ho gaya … aaj ka meter reading lelegiega… aaur bahar biometric mai bhaiya ka id bana hai register mai aab roz aane jaane ka entry hoga …."

"Theek hai …."

"Hum sham ko lautenge … laao room ki chabi hume dedo …."

Then, at about 1 pm they walk to Ellen building to attend the orientation session.

Massive amount of chairs line the hall with fancy taglines and boards on the stage … looks like a concert but ironically of the legacy of the coaching institutes and their results.

The director of the institute addresses the audience joined by some other HOD.

He sings the song "ye to sach hai ke bhagwan hai ……..mata pita…."

And then goes on with the well scripted and rehearsed speech ……

People clap and leave in an orderly manner.

Neelanshu, collects the study material, umbrella, ID card, all well branded with the institute's name.

At about 4:30 in the evening, they reach back to the hostel room …it is also snacks and tea time in the hostel mess …

"Chalo beta admission bhi ho gaya aab, mummy ko phone karlo …. Mujhe bhi nikalna hai eek ghante mai…"

"tayaari kar leta hun mai bhi."

He nods, while opening the latch of that brown door that opens into his room no. 105.

His Father packs up all the necessary things back into his red bag …. And says   "beta I will go… you stay in the hostel and as this is totally a new place for you… returning from the station alone will be a difficult task, may be you will get confused…."

"But, Papa …. I want to come …"

"No beta… You stay!"

6 o clock, Neelanshu escorts the bags of his Father, he hands 500 rupee note to Prajapati, and tells him to look after his son….

Auto stops in front of the hostel gate ….

"Kaha jana saab?" Sound comes from inside the vehicle

"Station" "Railway…?"

"Han baitho, 150 dedena…."

He touches the feet of his Father ….. Tears in his eyes are ready to roll down ….he tries pretend not to cry, stretching his retracting facial muscles and waves goodbye …. The auto starts, leaving his eyes with watery vision.

He rushes inside his room…. The feeling of being alone suddenly hits his conscience, he starts to cry.

His Father, also just leaves a text message that the train has set off to Patna… as he also cannot talk on the phone, with tears in eyes and heavy voice. His father gazes outside and flashbacks of his son appear in his mind.

On the study table a Hanuman Chalisa and a packet of chips are kept for him.

With the hope for tomorrow's class, he goes to sleep with, lights on, and dry marks of tears still on his cheeks.

9.

The keypad phone starts ringing and on its little screen, "Maa" flashes ….

He receives the phone call …

"Uth ja beta class hai na aaj … 6 bje …?"

"Han maa…."

"All the best … aake phone karna."

"Thiq hai maa … bye"

He gets off his bed and makes it …. Goes to the washroom take a chilly shower…. Takes out the new uniform of his institute, wears it …. Takes the notepad and puts module no 1 of bio 2 of physics and 1 of physical chemistry in his bag.

Combs in front of mirror …. Smiles and goes out of his room to fill the water bottle ….

6 am and the hostel mess already sounds of utensils, chatters, heavy shoes, with the smell of poha and tea, he stands in the line to take plate and spoon ,fills his plate with poha , sits at a corner ,eats … then moves out of the hostel gate ….

"Aare bhaiya…. Entry toh kariye …" says Prajapati sitting near the gate

"Han vo… mai bhul gya …."

 Neelanshu writes the information of his whereabouts in the thick ruled register, with that pen chained to a thread at its tail, lying besides.

At every right angle of the street students are seen crossing paths some in cycles some walking … Neelanshu walks in the direction of his institute, on the dried, cold, dusty streets….

He reaches the building …. Ascends the staircase just leading to a channeled gate …. First … second, third and finally fourth floor…

Students are queued in front of a strange box…. He also joins ….

Well, it is the electronic attendance machine …. In which students punch their id card's barcode and a green message- "Go" flashes on its display ….. Strange! But still, not foolproof.

"Chalo bacchon …." Says, a man wearing blue security formals ….

"Notice board mai time table laga dia hai …. Har roz ye change hoga … apne teacher ke naam bhi dekh le aaur koi problem ho to, batch mentor se mile…"

"Bina ID card aaur uniform ke aandar nahi aane dia jayega…"

And he leaves …. Meanwhile, everyone just settles into their class…

He enters room no 4, its heavy soundproof door with a little glass interface creaks every time students enter …. The classroom is huge; imagine it to be like a big matchbox in dimensions with low ceiling….. It is occupied with black steel long benches, leaving no rows or columns, somehow congested …. Equipped with duct air system, fans with rod and led on the ceiling. The front 3 rows have already been occupied one hour prior to the class starts, by some over enthusiastic kids. Neelanshu settles himself at a corner of 6th bench, it is already stuffed …. The class has the occupancy of almost 100 students but in reality, due to excess influx of admissions and aspiration each class contains 150 to 200 students , even when the city has more than 12 buildings of medical branch, each building has more than 6 floors … each floor has two sections, girls and boys separate, in case of medical …. Each section has 4 classes engaged with one in the morning shift from 6am to 2pm, and second from 2:30 to 8 pm …. This gives a glimpse, of the number of students, number of dreams, and at last- the most important number to the institute…. It's turnover!

There is this elevated platform, for teachers with a stretched whiteboard, covering 75 percent of the wall with watermarks of black, blue and red marker sketch of that previous class …. Below the board there is a duster kept and marker pens.

Adjacent to the board there are two posters, with lyrics written on them as …

"Itni shakti hume dena data….manka ….."

And other with the oath … that the institute wants you to recite everyday ……..

6 am sharp …. The bell rings…

"Itni shakti hame…. Daataaa aaaa …" brassy sound covers the class … from the speakers mounted on the corners of the classroom ……. A teacher enters the class in white shirt and brown pant …. Fixing a microphone on his nape and ear …..

He continues the prayer…

"Man ka viswash kamzor ho na……." and gestures the class, to stand up and join him in that hymn …

He points to that poster where it is written …

Now in unison, the sound becomes louder…

"Hum na sooche hame kya mila hai……"

Everyone sings ….until, the last stanza finishes.

The teacher tells them to settle down …

He clears his throat …. And jarring sound from the speaker comes…

"Haan to baccha kese ho aap log … mera naam MKG hai mai aapko cell biology padhaunga.. phela din h … accha yaha pr kitne bacche Bihar se hai?" … 60 percent of the class raises hands … then there are

Bengalis ,North Indians, people from South India, Punjab, Kashmir and North East, as well …. The class is really diverse.

"I am from Madhya Pradesh ….. Last year rank 1, 5, and 7 (writes) on the board mere hi shishya the … 15 saal ho gaye mujge padhate hue … chaliye all the best …"

"Aur han eek baat yaad rakhiye ….."

"Ncert aapka bhagwan hoga ….. No distractions ……class miss nahi karni…. rank laani hai"

"Chaliye heading daliye ….."

And he dictates the first line ….

"Cell is the basic structural –"

"Robert Hooke" ….."Micrographia" ……. And all the boys write in their spiral notepads …. With colorful pens … neat underlines …… the 1 hour 30 minute lecture ends with a bell.

The teacher leaves and instantly he is surrounded by students with their doubts….

Now, there will be a break of 10 minutes ….

Almost everyone moves out from the class and it is crowded, outside there is a cubicle at each floor which caters samosa chips patties at every 10 minute break …. It is already jammed ….

If you buy a seven rupee samosa , with a 10 rupee note, you get three toffees in return … for a 20 rupee note, you get thirteen toffees in return … now matter what! These vendors have never got change to return in monetary currency …..

The periphery of the walls outside the class is lined with notice boards all over …. With schedules major minor test ranks … results ….daily time table

Neelanshu tolls a bit … and sees the time table … and the names of teachers written as "K.P.Y" physics,

"S.G" biology, "Y.S" chemistry…

He asks… the floor in charge, "What does "P.K.G" in front of subjects denote…?"

"Aree beta S.G Sameer Gupta sir … aur P.K.G Pyush Kumar Gusain sir …"

"Simple."

His hand starts paining he has never written continuously for so long …. But he has to catch up … with the teachers pace.

All the remaining three lectures finish at 1:45, and the bell rings, Y.S sir says, "chalo kal ke lie heading dalo"

"IUPAC Nomenclature".

Stand up everyone, and take the oath before leaving the class....

"Mai prateegya karta hun ..."

And then students repeat ... following him

"Kathin paristhitiyon ka saama karte hue ... drin aatma vishwas aaur kadi nishta k saath ......"

And then everyone leaves making sounds of closing zips of their bags ... benches also relax making that metallic crux sound .....waiting for the next batch to come.

It is 45 degrees outside ....he opens the umbrella ... mini vans pickup ... autos, cycles ,crawl at a slow pace through roads ....

While returning towards the hostel ... many touts, hand students pamphlets either of some pg, hostel mess, or some coaching class....

He reaches his room sweating, irritation on his eyes prevail, due to dust .... He goes immediately to take a shower.

Changes .... Goes to the mess for lunch comes back .... Sits on the chair ... and takes a nap ....

Calls his father... "Ring" sound loops.

His father receives the call...

"Pranaam Papa... phauch gaye the?"

"Jeete raho Nishu ... han phauch gaya tha ... tum batao kesa gaya phela din? ... sab samaj mai to aya nah ... kuch samajh mai naa aae to teacher se puch lena ghabrane ki koi baat nahi hai ...."

"Haan papa ... din accha tha ... yahan pe bhaut acche teachers hai .... Par bheed bhaut hai ....garam bhi hai .... Aur baaki sab accha hai.."

" Accha chalo be hydrated ... talk to your Mother"

"Han beta Nishu Kesa hai?"

"Mai theeq hun tume miss kar raha hu ...."

"Hum bhi thume miss kar rahe hain ... acche se padhai karo beta .... Aar khane peene ka dhayan rakho ... thumara zyada time waste nahi karege aab tum padhai karpo ... chalo bye....."

He takes out the note book from his bag .... And start to revise.

10.

There are sporadic knocks on the door….

Neelanshu gets up from the study table … and opens it.

"Hi my name is Aviral…. Room no. 104 we are in the same batch I saw you in the class."

"Hahaha…. Ok come inside …" Neelanshu shakes hands with him … and offers him to sit on the chair, he has in his room.

 "Neelanshu …. From Patna …"

"Great …. I am from Bhilai Chattisgarh …. Tum, "N.T.S.E", yaa "K.V.P.Y" qualified ho …?

" Mera to 3 rd stage tak qualified hai …. Aur biology olympiad bhi ….."

Neelanshu never knew about such exams ….

He asks … "ntse matlab…?"

Aviral looks at him with a strange look… and bites his lips.

"Are…come its snacks time … chalo saath mai khalete hai."

They take chowmin from the mess counter and sit facing each other … till now everyone in the hostel is familiar with each other's faces….

"Aaur ncert le lia?" Asks aviral

"Nahi … Ellen ka material hai to…"

"Hahaha….. bhai ncert bhi padhna padhega …. Mera bhai jo abhi medcial college mai hai … usne pura ncert Ellen, vakash hcverma, barihant physics aur inorganic ak jagarwal kia …. Hume bhi karna padhega…. Samjhe? Nahi lia hai to mere saath "Friend's Bazaar" chalo sham ko … muje bhi books lene hai … tum bhi lelena……"

"Ok …. I will be ready in 20 minutes then."

Aviral comes in his room wearing a red T shirt "COOL" written on it, with white colored text… and brown shorts…. With the same coaching bag … in that too, he has written his name, address, roll number … and his full bio data….

"Let's go …"

Both … fill the entry register and walk towards friends bazaar, the golden sky is soothing …… the massive building of " gresonance" on the way reflects the golden hue of the sun streak upon eyes and faces.

The city mall, like twin rings, looks vibrant and attractive … with digital screens flashing advertisements…

They reach friends bazaar entrance … and the first block is of books … here you can purchase used new and antique books….

"Bhaiya ncert …. 11 ka do set "

They keep the books inside the bag …. Have ice-creams outside …. And with that of a brink left on the ice-cream cone, they also reach their hostel rooms.

He is somehow glad! That Aviral is his neighbor.

11.

Next day both go together …. Towards the class

It is their second day of class and there is some schedule updated on the notice board …… it says

This is to inform all the students that, they have to submit their school documents. Kindly, handover 10th mark sheets and pass certificate after the board results are out.

At the floor counter, they are also provided with list of schools nearby ….. These have same fees … although these do exist physically, but no one actually attends them… famous with the name "dummy schools". Only that you have to visit the school to write your 12th assignments and board examination.

Neelanshu keeps the list in his pocket; the class starts to sing "itni shakti hame-….." As the organic chemistry teacher enters into the class…. He also rushes inside.

Aviral tells him a rule …. Before entering the class …

"Friendship class ke bahar …."

And he sits on one extreme of the 7th row… while Neelanshu on the other….

Although Aviral was rude but Neelanshu did respected him for that.

At the beak time they fill water from the taps …. Outside the classroom

"Aaur, kaunsa school lene ki sochi hai?"

"Koi bhi, kya farak padhta hai… tu kaunsa leera hai …"

"Chal hostel p discuss karte hai ye baat …." Says Aviral, while, sipping water from his heavy Milton thermosteel.

Neelanshu "nods."

Remaining Classes resume.

12.

Knock! Knock!

"Open the door yaar Neelanshu …"

"It's me… Aviral at the door …"

"Han bhai wait … just coming I am in the washroom …"

He opens the door …..

"Come sit…"

"So, what have you decided …. School kahan lena hai …? Asks Aviral"

"tu jahan lega, mai bhi vahi le lunga …" both laugh

"I am planning to do dummy schooling from Delhi ….."

"Are you mad …?" Says Neelanshu

"Bhai ….. Here's the deal"

"If you do your schooling from Delhi …. Then you get a whopping 85% quota …"

"For instance when my brother gave the med exam … his All India Rank was around 700 it was impossible for him to get a college in centre, as the closing rank was 150 or something … but, as he did his schooling from that place … he got admitted easily …"

"You see if you are a topper … then this can make the cake sweeter!"

"Then what about the assignments? And board exam…"

"See full marks in practical from the school … you just have to give the exam that's all…"

"All the rankers have this Delhi schooling as a secret ingredient, to their success…"

"That's great … I will talk to my Father … regarding this…"

"IUPAC, bhi padhna hai … chal tell me tomorrow … byee.. And Aviral goes out of the room without shutting the door …"

"Hello Papa …vo….Aviral …"

"Yes what Aviral… you had a fight with him or what … should I talk to his dad-"

"Are no… listen to me first …"

"He was referring to some dummy schooling in Delhi … and that will be beneficial at the time of admission …"

"What is the problem in doing schooling from Kota? It is also dummy …"

"Areee.. Papa I will not get quota in Kota"

"Quota in Kota? What are you talking about…?"

"Taking admission in Delhi … we get 85% quota … that is during seat allotment priority will be given"

"Oh … we will see … when is the last date for 11th admission … ask your friend …"

"Ok I will let you know."

And he hangs up the phone.

Next day … after the cell biology class …. They eat samosa, again get toffees in return.

"Aviral where is that school you were talking about …?"

"That is in Delhi … only"

"Are tell … I won't tell it to anyone…"

"Sure? This thing will stay between us …. You see I don't want to make my competitors at par …."

"Han tell…"

"It is in Dwarka …."

"New Hope Public School"

"What sort of a name is that …."

"What's in a name … see the results … all the toppers as they claim were from that school …see Google it"

"Hahah…. But look you will soon find a loop"

"I don't have time for searching ….. All this"

"Bhai… Most of them were Ellen classroom students…"

"See?"

The bell rings and kinematics lesson starts.

After the classes get over they enter the hostel mess to have lunch….

"Neelanshu I will talk to my Father so may be your Father can also accompany him …for our admission… what say?"

"Han that would be efficient enough…"

And both go into their room ……

13.

While revising the black stick compounds of organic chemistry he falls asleep … the chill of the air conditioner wakes him up.

Still in a distorted sense of time, until he reaches outside of his hostel, the Sun is almost about to set …. It's a beautiful evening but crowed.

He decides to buy patties from somewhere nearby … fills the entry register.

As you walk on the streets in the evening time, you could see a totally different phase radiating up a totally different vibe …. The students now walk, hand in hand … some return from their classes, some just fill up the voids, to pass time in the parks …. Some stressed, happy … lost, and you can see what you want … the scenario at the streets can be a reflection of your inner self.

Shops lit up with colorful lights, ice-cream stalls, the infamous cyber cafes, where you can find all sorts of movies ….. They offer 5 movies in 10 rupees…

Cyber cafes with names such as "Chaska" … "Khandelwal" etc, are big eye catchers and always crowed… with people coming for different motives … some passing time by playing videos … gaming ….. Others are here to fill some competitive forms ….. Altogether, cyber cafes are a major hangout point for students where they get diverted in a massive way. This eventually will be your first step towards self destruction and cyber addiction ….

There are also shacks where tea and cigarettes are being sold ….. Barely 17 or 18 these young ones curse themselves with dose of smoke tar daily.

This darker side of the place resides with welcoming hands, the choice is totally yours!

Neelanshu, reaches a stall …. Already flooded with fast food orders …

He sees the menu …. "Patties", "masala patties", "maonese patties"… and so many of them … Maggie … "masala maggie"… so on… he orders for a "masala patties …"

"Pack kardo" and he takes the package.

While eating patties in his room … his phone "Rings"

"Han papa.. pranaam ."

"Beta kese ho … Aviral ke papa aaur mai Delhi mai hai thumara dono ka admission ho gaya hai …."

"Thanks … ye to accha hai"

"Han hum aaj yahi rehenge .. Delhi mai hi … chalo dhyan rakho bye."

He gets up from his room, then rushes to room no 104 …

Bhai admission finally ho gaya …both overlap each other's statements, and laugh out while shaking hands.

14.

The tide of admission is now at low ebb … now tide is high for preparation. Those really willing, have hectic days with Sundays left to revise.

Today even the morning is hot and humid …. And the class feels suffocating too, with handkerchief and water bottles handy.

Meanwhile, someone enters the class with a slip in his hands …. He goes to the teacher teaching at the platform and shows him the instruction.

 The class fills in with murmurs of suspicion.

"Baccho khuskhabri hai aap sab ke lie…" says M.K.G sir…

Everyone start ranting …

"Quiet …"

"You will have your first minor test this Sunday … of "NEET" pattern"

Everyone listens attentively…

"Hmm…. That will be of 720 marks in which each section of biology zoology physics and chemistry will have 45 questions each …"

"180 question hai 3 ghante … dekhte hai kaun top 20 mai aata hai."

"Chaliye revise kariye ga… test schedule venue aaur timing noticeboard se dekh leegiyega."

"All the best"

The class cheers up in excitement …

Today even in the breaks, most were into their notes … Saving time for the upcoming exam.

While having lunch …. Aviral says

"Exam tak mujhse koi baat mat karna… theek hai ?"

Neelanshu stares and freezes with roti in his hands… laughs and says..

"Theek hai! All India rank 'one'."

Before these major tests, those who study even forget to breathe …. But miracle of this place is that those who don't, somehow they also- at least talk about studying and strategizing plans.

15.

A message pops out in his cell phone…

From, ELLENMEDICAL

Dear Neelanshu, classroom student of Ellen Institute, kindly report fifteen minutes prior to the exam, at the decided venue. Timings will be 10 am to 1 pm, at block 1, room no 5.

Please bring your ID card in the exam hall.

All the best!

A day before exam, the atmosphere at the hostel is supplemented with talks of upcoming exam bouncing wall to wall…. Rooms latched from inside … lesser people for dinner … you know how it is one day before the exam … situation is almost the same universally.

Students are already buzzing near the aqua guard …. 5:30 in the morning … some just woke up to revise, while some will now go to sleep, after an eye popping one night toil.

Neelanshu, also wakes up… calls his Mother …and talks to her for a while… she wishes him good luck for the exam.

9:15 am almost everyone is having their breakfast … and revising there itself… Lesser chatter prevails.

Here people revise from the mnemonics not from the notes … as class notes are already piled up making hills in the room.

He fills up the entry register rushes and shares the auto till block 1 …

ID card?

He shows the ID card to the invigilator in the exam hall… the invigilator directs him to his seat … where his roll number is written.

Students still keep on coming.

Bundles of orange sheets and red omr answer sheets are distributed to all ….

The invigilator announces … and guides everyone to fill their omr sheets …

Most fill wrong dots …. Or overdo them; the invigilator distributes new sheets to them.

Here you can do as many mistakes as you want … but remember, in the main examination there will be only one answer sheet … and no excuses…

"Now you can open the seal of your question paper and start reading …" says the invigilator while writing the date on the whiteboard.

After filling some dots on the o.m.r … most in the bio section, then the chemistry and almost none in the physics … rechecks the answers.

Some "meritorious" students fill the o.m.r fully and randomly ….. At last they are seen making designs on their question paper….

The bell rings...

The sheets are collected by the invigilator....

Just in front of the exam hall .... A cubicle is set up to distribute the exam solution and answer key ...

All students mutter outside ... matching their answers ... like "phele ka (b) ... dusree ka (a)"... and so on

He reaches the hostel room ... switches off the lights and goes to sleep.

Snacks time and he wakes up.... Aviral knocks at his room ...

"How was the exam?"

"Bhai pata nahi .... I am expecting between 300-400 ... what about you?"

"Han 550 shayad..."

"Party fir toh ..... Says Neelanshu!"

"Haan let's see .... 7 o clock taka a jayega result."

"Both go to have tea."

"The results are out check on the website..." says Aviral

Neelanshu gives his roll number to him and they both wait for the site to open ....

Biology 170/360 physics 12/180 chemistry 33/180

Class rank 700

Phase rank 1234

He gets baffled by the scores in chemistry and physics.... feels sad and disappointed too... as he did a lot of negative marking.

Aviral opens his scorecard...

Biology 320/360 physics 154/180 chemistry 156/180

Class rank 4

Phase rank 12

The results of these tests can raise barriers, define standards, create or destroy, build you up, make you stronger or leave you shattered.... This is what the first test can do to your psyche.

After the Sunday exam, there is chill atmosphere everywhere irrespective of the results .... The parks blossom with cricketers, footballers and lovers.

The cyber café is stuffed with movie buffs....

And food chains are busy serving nonstop orders.

16.

Aviral's passport size photo is studded in the notice board; after all he is one of the top twenty rankers.

Class starts with daily chores ...

SG sir enters the class…. He tells the top 20 rankers to stand …

Of which 6 are from his batch ….

He gives a parker to the rankers , Aviral is lucky enough to get one …The pen, however just a pen, it can act, also as a psychological fuel that can boost anyone to strive harder ahead…

Other 140 guys sitting in the class just dream as spectators …. Neither happy, nor sad, just eyeing the pen…

Studies resume.

The top rankers are later filtered from the batch and sent to special rank batch as they call it, these students are an asset to the institute and they take great care of them as well …. By providing them with room at hostel … doubt clearing teachers on call… And, what not …!

But what about the other students who are here to learn, to improve, to seek for guidance, are they just to fill the benches? Or support the economy? Or are they just mere roll numbers… in that rank section…?

In this battle system of rank, special batch makes one doubt self…. anxious and far from the real knowledge…. Critical thinking fades away sooner or later … personality flips massively … your vision becomes myopic.

Some become so engrossed in this process that they forget the outside world …. They forget that life is also about music, compassion, dreams, senses, expression, emotions, landscapes, seasons, exploration, art, possibilities; they forget that life is also about living.

17.

Here in Kota, mornings have taken a totally different toll ….

Now, there are only thunders of alarms ringing as early as 3 am …. Also the walls have no more the posters of rock bands neither the ceilings host colorful led.

The scenario has changed so much, that now the plain walls have long charts, pasted with formulas, diagrams chemical compounds….

Deadlines written … motivational quotes filling up the spaces on the study table… names etched and carved on that wooden head of the bed with compass "rank 1" written everywhere… maybe this is how a room in Kota looks like… wait there's even more to that … wooden racks are now filled with coaching sheets some pending others finished … extra heavy objective books ….

In the washroom the mirror has also lost its charm … it too speaks the language of biology physics and chemistry …..

That is how deep you have to drown to swim one day.

Neelanshu carries off with the regular schedule ….though it has now become a bit mechanical.

In the mornings the maid knocks you off your sleep, by literally playing drums at your door … sometime when you miss the cleanliness routine and then your room is filled with all sort of dust and dirt, the dustbin is ready to puke with its mouth open…. And then, you discuss with your hostel mates…." Aaj safai wali didi aai thi kya?" … some people will still say proudly "mera room toh eek hafte se saaf nahi hua"….

Neelanshu, is totally stirred up in this ambience ….

Today is the last Sunday of the month and as usual it is a rule that there will be no dinner served in the hostel …it will be a rest day for the mess workers.

Neelanshu heads off to the mess… And there is no one there…

He then realizes the issue ….

However, he is not alone…. Pratham that "JEE" guy from the 2nd floor is also there…

Pratham, invites him to have green tea…he agrees …as it is too late to have dinner anywhere outside … and he is already feeling full, it's after a long time since he will have a conversation with someone.

Sitting in an awkward silence, well something was missing today; they could totally not relocate the topic to speak.

"My engineering is screwed up", says Pratham while boiling water in that electric kettle…..

Neelanshu asks him, "why?"

May be he wanted to share something … or so

"Hahaha….. Man! As soon as I leave this place I am going to visit a psychiatrist …."

"Look brother", hands him the tea…

"It's been two years in Kota, I have been totally unstable, and be it emotionally or mentally."

"I have developed a fear of accidents , I think that everything that's around me is going to harm me … and ultimately I will die…I don't know where to seek support from ….I am in such a state where my mind produces negative thoughts only …"

Sighs …

"I have missed a lot of opportunities till now, because of this thing which I have in me…"

"For instance, when I dress up for the class … walk up to the door … then "tinggg" my mind gets hit with fear and anxiety ….. You know I usually faint whenever I over think, once, it happened at the railway station and then when I came back to the room boom! I fainted once again …

You know I have never told this thing to anyone … not even to my parents… And today speaking my heart out to a totally stranger … please don't mind haan bro…

Sometime I get so depressed that to overcome it I sleep, I sleep a lot … to escape time… often days pass locked inside the room, without food, no human interaction ….developed a caffeine addiction…here, and I am telling you all this because it is not my fault … it is the ignorance of this place that works in a spotlight manner … only the stars are portrayed while there is so much of the darkness to look after ….

You are lucky … at least your parents call you …

It's been a month since I have talked to mine ….. Maybe all this has made me what I am today.

Neelanshu says nothing …. He is intrigued to see, that life in his hostel, lie beyond books also …

Calls his mom, and goes to sleep thinking about the guy's situation.

This is the beauty of Kota … where there are "Avirals" there are "Prathams" also … and in between there are "Neelanshus" too… with starting points the same, and endings totally diverse.

19.

ICSE board results are out …no one really cares though in this competitive exam oriented city about the percent … here people with percent as low as 55 make it to IIT or AIIMS .

Still people getting 95% in board exams, in rest of the country lag way behind in this game of ticking the correct one, from the four options given.

Neelanshu has scored 78%....

Today his Father has credited 1000 rupees in his account … he plans to give a treat to Aviral this evening…

They go to the famous "Punjabi Dhabha" … order a thali … eat and come back grabbing paneer rolls from the "rolls hub" restaurant …. They delight their taste buds after a long time …

In the evening the same day …. Now they both go back to study … as instant gratification is not their way of enjoying things.

There is a knock at the door ….

"Laundry bhaiya laundry …."

Once a week the laundry guy comes, and takes all your dirt to wash off …. From bed sheets to towels everything that you have either stained or giving it for a rewash, just for the sake of it.

Except, the undergarments you can give everything … and while collecting, the guy jots down in a register … the collar of your cloth has your room number written on it, with that black permanent marker.

Once, a guy in the hostel gave his underwear in the laundry …. Guess what happened next?

An epidemic broke out! with most suffering from fungal infection. All gross in the groin … itchy life… until, tubes were distributed in the hostel …as the ultimate savior.

Students mostly suffer from diarrhea, fever, food poisoning, indigestion, depression, home sickness and a plethora of other diseases…. The physical ones are treated, but mental ones remain dormant untreated for lifelong.

20.

Around five months have passed here … with the same routine and quarterly tests … Aviral still tops the exam, while Neelanshu improves slowly with each exam … at his own pace

The feeling of competition and jealously, has somehow set in between the two …

Today, Neelanshu is gripped by the fever as rainy season has started ….

He missed the class… Aviral denies him to share the class notes…

There are students that just punch the identity cards in the attendance machine and never attend the class …. They just dress up from the hostel and go to the coaching building to just mark the attendance … and fool their parents…. You will find many such people there.

The sixth major tests results are out, and this time Neelanshu has managed to score well in the examination … while Aviral's performance has dipped very hard.

It is Neelanshu's turn to take the pen from SG sir….

He is happy … today at least he got a little hope…

They both don't talk much … even meals are eaten separately …. They both have now set a common goal- to get ahead of each other.

In the further tests, there is again rise in Neelanshu's performance while Aviral fails to coup up with the marks.

Nelanshu's photo gets into the notice board section while, Aviral struggles to get even rank in top 500.

This, triggers a cold war between the two … further they both stop talking.

Three weeks later …..

It is Friday morning …. There is police at the hostel, In front Aviral's room.

There are exhaustive knockings on the door …. Still, there is no response from inside.

Whole floor is crowded … the inspector instructs the warden to break the door and … puts handkerchief on his nose instantly ….

Neelanshu, rushes to see what has happened … and there they see, Aviral hanging from the ceiling fan … dead still.

His room smells of the rotten dead ….. The dead body is taken off from the fan, it is then covered with the blood stained bed sheet.

No notes left, not any quarrels with anyone…. Still he commits suicide.

Neelanshu is disturbed by the incident, and he is sort of numb too, smoldering flashes of memories pollute his conscience ….

 The inspector interrogates him.

Aviral's father arrives crying ….. Kneels down on the floor beating his head …

He is then comforted with a glass of water … and then the inspector in charge tells him and the hostel owner, to give permission for autopsy in the police station.

Next day, the autopsy reports are out by the forensic department ….

That guy brutally killed himself …. First he overdosed with some amphetamines …. Then made a cut on his wrist... And at last, he hanged himself to death.

Three days, he was inside that room … no one bothers about him, neither the parents, the hostel warden, either the friends, nor the coaching.

There is no one to blame in such cases … the reason and root cause remains unaltered.

Days pass… within a week students leave the hostel …. The owner organizes a shanti path in the hostel, prasaad is served and holy water is sprinkled at every corner.

No one roams around after 10 pm, even the mirror in lift is removed, and instead a poster with pictures of god is pasted there ….

True satire with someone's coffin!

Those who witnessed the incident will remain scarred for life …. It has really impacted their perception.

Although Neelanshu now, tries keeping up with the pace to study

Three months later.

21.

Neelanshu is scoring well in the tests, it is also his board class this year and he will sit for medical entrance simultaneously.

Today, list of students selected for special rank batch is getting displayed on the notice board …. And his name is also there.

 SG sir enters the class…. And announces the names of students selected.

"You people have to grab a rank no matter what … hardly 7 months left study hard, and those lagging behind please improve, please assemble for the award distribution , the top rankers will get a silver medal."

Neelanshu, gets a silver medal, from the coaching for his impeccable performance … in that massive gathering of the students.

The mentor of their batch, hands him the list and extra class timings for the special batch … and they get a hamper written on it with red "TARGET AIIMS".

Special batch classes have already stared…

There are around 20 students in there …..

As the ultra competitive and mind storming class gets over, all are dismissed by the teacher… they head outside the class…

"Hey listen … hey you!"

As he walks out from the building block, some girly sound travels in his direction…

A girl taps him on his back…

"Excuse me … yes; what can I do for you?" He says to her…

"Idiot … you left off your ID card in the class…"

She hands him the ID card …

He takes it …and smiles

"By the way I am also in special rank batch …. Prior to this mes5a rank 3."

"Wow That's great!" says Neelanshu.

"Thanks then …."

"Wait your name again?"

"Sathwikta…."

"And you are Neelanshu right?"

He nods, blushes and both move in opposite directions, adjusting the straps of their heavy bags.

22.

Days get up more tied up by the time pinching schedule.... His world revolves around classes....

Ignited and confident, he performs well in the daily tests...

In the periodic special rank tests, Sathwikta still leads ahead …

Neelanshu's Father, informs him in the phone that he will have to report at the school in Delhi in order to submit project files and give practical…

Next day, he leaves off to Delhi …via train … he reaches the "Ramakrishna Metro Station" … with bags and piles of books … gets to see people from outside world after a long time … swipes the metro coin at "Dwarka Metro Station"….hires an auto towards "New Hope Public School."

Many students have reported … some are still on their way … he submits the files …. Gets over with all the assignments, and prepares to return to Kota the same evening.

While sitting in the train, he gets a text

"Hi! Sathwikta here …. Hope you are fine …. I have photocopied all the notes for you… of today's class … will see you tomorrow. Best of journey!"

He texts back…

"Thanks! But where did you get my number from?"

She replies…

"From your ID card …"

Next day, at about 5 am he reaches Kota … and enters his room …. Takes a bath and gets ready to attend the classes.

Sathwikta, hands him over the notes … he smiles, and asks her out for snacks.

After their special batch group class, they eat patties and coffee… with talks as dessert and sweetness of innocence as toppings to it.

One more test and this time he scored more than Sathwikta….

She calls him on the phone, congratulates him …

"So … tomorrow is Sunday … what are you doing?" Asks Neelanshu

"Nothing much … will go to big bazaar … to buy some stuff" she says…

"Let's catch up then … even I have to buy some …"

"Ok 1 in the noon then?"

"Done?"

"Yup see you!"

Hangs up the line….

The other day, 12 pm … 4 missed calls from Sathwikta … he sees and calls back instantly … apologizes for not receiving the call, she scolds him ….

They decide to meet within an hour near the city mall….

Neelanshu gets ready wearing casuals after a long time; he wears a blue T shirt teamed up with denims…. Fills the entry register and takes the auto…

Sathwikta wearing white top and blue denims has already arrived holding an empty bag….

The city mall of Kota is a hub, always lively …. It carries an aroma of its own within, as you enter … you see mostly students some with their parents while most with their friends or partners.

They both don't talk much though … a little awkwardness still bridges them …

Before entering the big bazaar section, they hand over their bags at the security …

He makes fun of her, as she comes to the mall with a shopping list … with even the slightest things vividly written on it, like a child.

They get over with the billing, and move out from the mall ….

3 pm …

"Bye then…" she says

"No, I think we should go to Seven Wonders … I have not explored this place, I will be happy if you join me…"

"We will be back till 5…"

Sathwikta … bites her lips in contemplation … and agrees.

"Two tickets …. 10 rupees" says the vendor sitting at the gate of Seven Wonders Park …

They enter the park … it is beautiful yet decent … with picturesque replicas of Seven Wonders of the World…

Visitors are clicking selfies … and group photographs…

"Idiot we even don't have a smart phone to click a picture …"

"Hmmm … wait I'll do something…"

He walks towards the periphery of the park where a photography stall is set up ….

They get a photograph clicked by the photographer and get it processed…. With a cliché move, they then tear it into half and exchange the pieces of the picture …

Before going to sleep….. Neelanshu texts her…

"Thanks … I enjoyed a lot today …"

She, texts back.

"Mee too … sleepwell."

23.

Four months left for the exam …. They usually meet on Sundays and talk on regular basis.

After a while they become good friends … dopamine levels on both their systems shoot up … they start to bunk classes , watch movies , dine inn ….

Their performance in the test, start to decline…. Further they get more close to each other.

She, proposes him … they get into a relationship, obsession overpowers.

They break up in a sudden turn of fluctuation…. He gets shattered … she tries to explain, either they can be with each other, or they can study.

She changes her path… Her phone number … there is no trace of her after that.

Weeping, he sits in his room ….shouts in agony, echoes surrounds his mind, chaining him to the thoughts of his "Parents"…. "Aviral" …. "Sathwikta" … his "rank" … "studies"…. All come in a spiral…

He latches the door from inside and tears up the pages of his books …. Throws all the furniture here and there ….. Makes his room like a destroyed garage … and sleeps in the piles of books there itself.

This was the episode of depression and anger he suffered from ….. The day before…

Now, he was fully in his senses somehow relaxed….

He gets up as if to start something new …. Smiles, bathes…. Sings…

Cleans his room …. And makes a commitment of never loosing track again …. He takes this as a revelation.

So much happens, but still he gathers the courage to move on…

Board exam dates are also announced by then…..

He is busy preparing for boards…. English is now a major headache for him, as he has not touched it since past 2 years.

Rest, the subjective description makes him wonder a lot …

He is presently webbed to all this only.

Board exam commence …. The subjective sheets look weird, although all exams were of medium difficulty….. He writes them well.

He is back to Kota …. Coaching classes resume…. The newspapers have headlines of the medical entrance exam forms….

Students rush to the cyber cafes, to get the form filled ….. There is enormous waiting to fill the form … to get passport size photographs processed … thumb impressions… Signatures….

Neelanshu , after waiting the whole day in the cyber café for his turn …. Gets done with filling the medical entrance registration form successfully….

The exam is to be held on 6th of May, as written on the crisp admit card …. That just incarnated from the printer.

24.

The day has finally come; two years of toil will be scaled against the three hours of exam.

6th of May …. Text messages from relatives and school friends flood his cell phone in the morning … he wonders how great caretakers and well wishers were some of them … just remembering his existence on the exam day.

"All the best beta accha jayega… thumara exam says his Mother, lo Papa se bhi baat karo aaur Gopal sir bhi aaye hai thume all the best bolne…."

He greets everyone on the phone and without talking much hangs it up.

Switches off the lights of his room …. Sits introspecting   … breathes calmly … grabs the admit card and locks his room …… fills the entry register ….

It is just like any other day ….. Masses are gathered to write the exam … they are being checked by the authorities…

Papers are distributed …. With the sound of fan … the bell rings and the battle starts.

The rawness of texture of that sophisticated question paper gets felt on the shivering fingers … while the smoothness of the pen is somehow relaxing.

It's almost time to wave a good buy to this place, each element has its own flavor here, each student has his own story, although still from outside, but randomness rules the aura…. acclimatization sets in automatically and your stay here passes, teaching you a lesson small or big ….

He packs up bundles of sheets …books …clothes… and piles them up at a corner of his room …. Seeing all this, he realizes that time really flies …. Adding up more to your subjective self … it could be with many imperfect edges however.

Putting the backpack in the auto, and holding Patna's returning tickets in his hands …. His stay in Kota has been minute and unnoticeable to anyone residing there …. There is no one to give him a farewell … only some memories and lessons.

Equilibrium will be maintained in this place forever…

Today when Neelanshu leave at this instant … someone just arrives here at another…

Kota will always be a place with numerous "Neelanshus", "Prathams", "Sathwiktas" and "Avirals"…..

Always…..and always….

Neelanshu scores well in the medical entrance examination …. He is being glorified all over, only he knows what nullness of ridicule he had to vacuum inside to get here.

Gopal sir comes to meet him with sweets… and hugs him…

He takes out a photo frame from his coaching bag …. Gives it to Gopal sir ….

"What is this that you are giving me…? Two photographs … in tattered state that too of two different people…. What will it be of my use?

Neelanshu smiles and answers …. Holding the frame in his hands…

"See this … He, is Aviral and points at the other half torn photo besides… she is Sathwikta….

"Where are they now?"

Neelanshu …. "Remains silent…."

Gopal sir … confused, accepts the gift from him…. Takes the frame home and cage it into the showcase of his living room…. it occupies space with no story to convey, just smiling faces, gazing through, peeping outside.

THE END